First published in 2018 by Scholastic Children's Books
Euston House, 24 Eversholt Street
London NW1 1DB
a division of Scholastic Ltd
www.scholastic.co.uk
London - New York - Toronto - Sydney - Auckland
Mexico City - New Delhi - Hong Kong

Text and Illustrations copyright © 2018 Sarah McIntyre

HB ISBN 978 1407 14329 3
PB ISBN 978 1407 14330 9

All rights reserved

Printed in Malaysia

13 5 7 9 10 8 6 4 2

The moral rights of Sarah McIntyre have been asserted.
Papers used by Scholastic Children's Books are
made from wood grown in sustainable forests.

The chief asked her lots of questions
to see if she might make a good firefighter.
Dipsy's heart went THUMPETY THUMP.
Would she... could she... get this job?

Hooray! Dipsy got the job. But becoming a firefighter wasn't easy.

All the uniforms were WAY too small and a grumpy firefighter had to order her a special big one.

XXXXXXXL

Dipsy had always wanted to slide down the pole...

"Please help me!" sobbed Mr Iguanodon.
"My little Snookums is stuck in a tree!"

"I can do this!"
said Dipsy.

Was this Dipsy's chance
to prove herself?

Her long neck was just right for reaching up to the top branch.

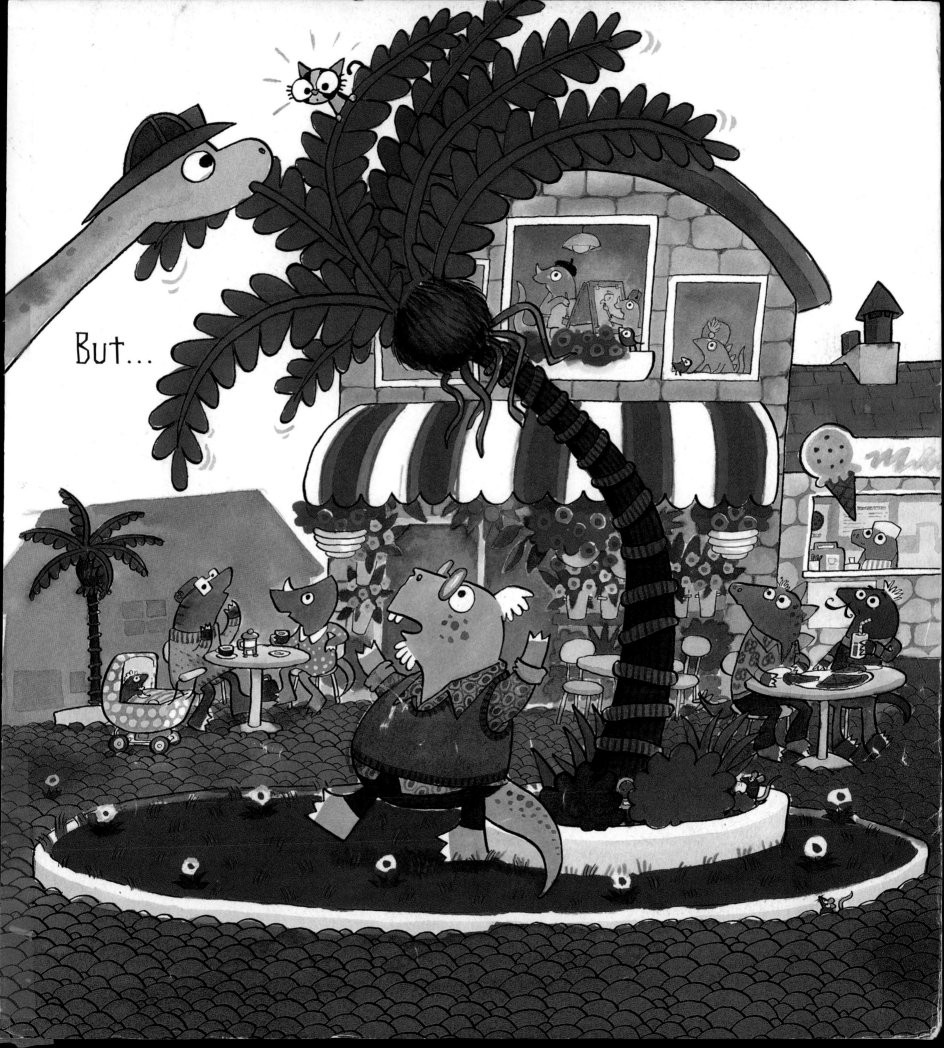

But...

Uh-oh! Dipsy pulled that branch **too** hard and the kitten flew through the air like a fluffy rocket...

... and crash-landed in the mayor's pudding with a...

SPLAT!!

"Whoopsie!" said Dipsy.
"I'm so, so, so sorry!"

NEE-NAR NEE-NAR

Dipsy didn't have much time to worry... they had another emergency!
"I won't mess things up this time!" she promised.

At the park, Trevor the T-Rex was stuck in the climbing frame.

Firefighter Jamie sighed, "Oh, Trevor, not AGAIN!"

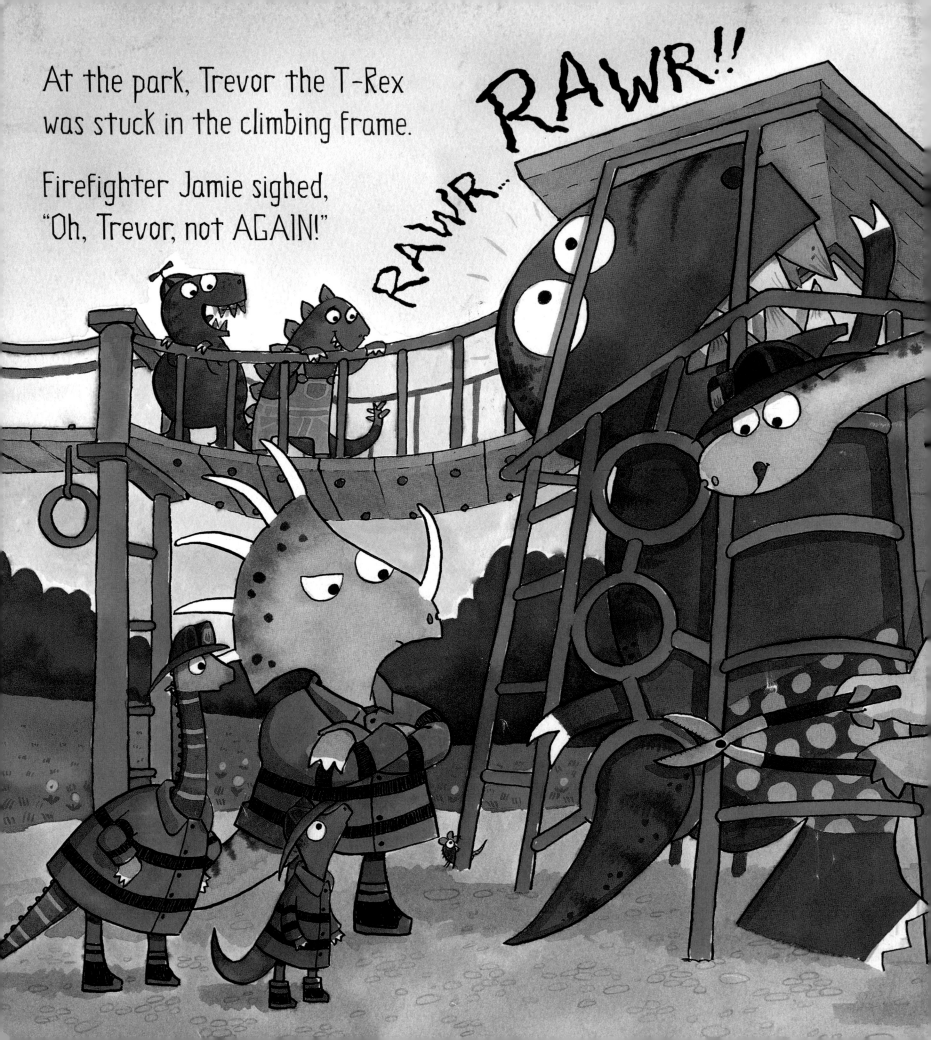

Dipsy cut through the metal climbing frame very, very carefully. But she was being SO careful that she didn't notice her tail flicking about...

Back at the fire station, Dipsy felt awful.
I'm the worst firefighter EVER, she thought. *I get everything wrong.*

But **leaping lizards!**
The fire engine had broken down. What a **disaster!**

Dipsy had an idea.
"I can be the fire engine!" she roared.
All the firefighters cheered
and jumped on her back.

NEE-NAR NEE-NEE-NAR!

Dipsy made the siren sound as they rushed to the rescue.

The town hall was saved. All the dinosaurs cheered and cheered.

OUR HERO!

The mayor was so happy, she gave Dipsy
a huge shiny medal.
"Hooray for Dipsy, this
town's finest fire engine...

...and the BEST firefighter!"